W9-AKE-695

WITHDRAWN

The Most Amazing Bird

For my irngutaq (granddaughter), Hazel,
who lives where this story takes place.
—M.A.K.

The Most Amazing Bird

written by Michael Arvaarluk Kusugak

illustrations by Andrew Qappik, CM

annick press

toronto • berkeley

Aggataa's feet went crunch, crunch, crunch
on the hard snow.

Crunch, crunch, crunch went her grandmother's feet.

"Anaanattiak, what is that bird?" asked Aggataa.

"It is a tulugarjuaq," her grandmother replied, "a raven."

"It's ugly. It looks like it slept in its coat," Aggataa said.

"And its coat is too big. Why is it still here? It's the middle of winter."

"Tulugarjuat are winter birds," her grandmother said.
"They stay here all winter. This one likes me.
It follows me everywhere."

"I don't like it. Go away, ugly bird!" Aggataa yelled.

"Crah!" answered the bird.

The next morning, Aggataa saw two ravens.

While one raven—a huge, ugly bird—teased the sled dogs, the smaller raven stole some of the dogs' food. Then off they flew, looping and somersaulting through the air.

After a few minutes, the birds started to fight. The big raven grabbed the stolen food and flew away.

"Mean bird!" Aggataa yelled at the huge bird.

"**Crah!**" the bird replied.

"Why is the small raven
always here, Anaanattiak?"
Aggataa asked.

"Last winter, when it first came, it was small and it was sick. I fed it. And it has stayed close to me ever since."

Anaanattiaq handed Aggataa some fish and said, "Take this outside and give it to him."

"Here, Ugly Bird!" Aggataa yelled.

The bird hopped over, took the fish, and hopped away with it. It began to eat but did not fly away. The big black bird watched from a distance.

"Naa, naa, na, nanny; you're not getting any," Aggataa teased the big raven.

"**Crah!**" the bird replied.

From then on, when Aggataa walked to her grandmother's hut, the small bird would meet her along the way.

"Hi, Ugly Bird," she would say.
And the bird would hop along behind her.

Soon the spring sun stayed up in the sky day and night and the snow softened.

The ravens still played, flying around doing loops and somersaults. Now, the frost was gone from their beaks. They were so black they looked almost blue. Their feathers glistened in the sun. And their coats were no longer too big. They fit.

Now, they were beautiful.

One sunny spring day, Aggataa saw a little bird, a round white bird with black wings: a qupanuaq, a snow bunting.

She watched as it flapped its wings and rose up then stopped flapping and dropped down. Up and down, up and down it flew.

The sandhill cranes came next. Flaa-ap, flaa-ap. Aggataa loved the extra little flap that they made with their long, graceful wings.

She watched them walk in the hills, holding up their long, thin necks. She heard them cry out, "**Krr-krr.**"

The seagulls arrived, too. They screamed, "**Squawk, squawk!**" They were always hungry and they were noisy. Aggataa did not like gulls. She liked quiet birds.

More birds arrived. Snow geese. Canada geese. Ducks.
Loons. Swans. Flocks of ptarmigans. Many different birds.

The birds built nests. Soon, there were little birds everywhere.

Little sigjariarjuit—sandpipers—just little tufts of gray fluff
with long, skinny legs ran about, falling over, getting up
and running again.

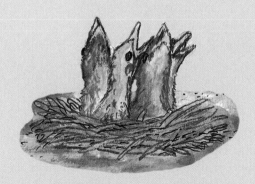

Pairs of swans floated peacefully
on the lakes with their little ones.

Aggataa looked for the ravens,
but they were nowhere to be found.

"Maybe the ravens have flown away,"
she thought. "What funny birds they are.
Why do they come here for the cold
winter and fly away when spring and
summer come?"

Before long, the grasses stood tall, waving in the late summer breeze. The birds gathered in great numbers.

Geese landed on the hillsides by the thousands.

The sandhill cranes floated into the sky with their young, teaching them how to fly.

Flocks of snow buntings flew around.

Soon, a thin layer of ice formed on the lakes every night, only to melt away during the day.

Aggataa watched the swans bob up and down among the waves.

Every day, all day long, Aggataa watched
long Vs of geese flying south.

Soon, the other birds began to fly away, too.

The little kajuqtaat, horned larks, were the last to go. As the snow came, the brown birds with black cheeks ran around in the drifts, looking for food.

Before long they too were gone. Winter had come.

Aggataa was sad. There were no more birds.

One day, as Aggataa was walking to her grandmother's hut, she heard an incredible sound: "**Crah!**"

Sitting on a rock was the
ugliest bird she had ever seen.

"Hi, Ugly Bird!" Aggataa yelled.

"**Crah!**" the bird replied.

It would not be a lonely winter after all.

The most amazing bird was back.

Taima

© 2020 Michael Arvaarluk Kusugak (text)
© 2020 Andrew Qappik, CM (illustrations)

Edited by Mary Beth Leatherdale

Cover art by Andrew Qappik, designed by Robin Mitchell Cranfield
Interior design by Robin Mitchell Cranfield

Annick Press Ltd.

All rights reserved. No part of this work covered by the copyrights hereon may be reproduced or used in any form
or by any means—graphic, electronic, or mechanical—without the prior written permission of the publisher.

We acknowledge the support of the Canada Council for the Arts and the Ontario Arts Council, and the participation
of the Government of Canada/la participation du gouvernement du Canada for our publishing activities.

Canada ❋

ONTARIO ARTS COUNCIL
CONSEIL DES ARTS DE L'ONTARIO
an Ontario government agency
un organisme du gouvernement de l'Ontario

Library and Archives Canada Cataloguing in Publication

Title: The most amazing bird / written by Michael Arvaarluk Kusugak ; illustrated by Andrew Qappik,
CM.
Names: Kusugak, Michael, author. | Qappik, Andrew, 1964- illustrator.
Identifiers: Canadiana (print) 20200189069 | Canadiana (ebook) 20200189093 | ISBN 9781773214184
(hardcover) | ISBN 9781773214214 (PDF) | ISBN 9781773214191 (HTML) | ISBN 9781773214207 (Kindle)
Classification: LCC PS8571.U83 M67 2020 | DDC jC813/.54—dc23

Published in the U.S.A. by Annick Press (U.S.) Ltd.
Distributed in Canada by University of Toronto Press.
Distributed in the U.S.A. by Publishers Group West.

Printed in China

annickpress.com
michaelkusugak.com

Also available as an e-book.
Please visit annickpress.com/ebooks for more details.